This book is dedicated to Jessica and Rebecca—
two of the very best reasons to visit Kansas.

Edited by Aileen Andres Sox
Designed by Dennis Ferree
Art by Mary Rumford
Typeset in 14/18 Weiss

ISBN: 0-8163-1123-4

93 94 95 96 97 • 5 4 3 2 1

Beautiful Bones and Butterflies

By Linda Porter Carlyle   Illustrated by Mary Rumford

Pacific Press Publishing Association
Boise, Idaho
Oshawa, Ontario, Canada

apa stops the car by the edge of the road. "Here we are," he says.

I take my big brown paper bag and climb out of the car. I stand still at the edge of the road. I listen to the quiet country sounds around me. I hear little insects buzzing in the grass.

I follow Papa into the field. "We're looking for milkweed," he says. "Come here. I'll show you what it looks like."

"Look," says Papa, pointing to a tall green plant. "Look closely."

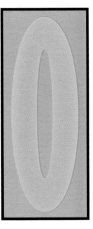-o-oh," I whisper. There on the milkweed I see one. A little black-and-yellow caterpillar. Then suddenly I see another one. And another.

Papa breaks off pieces of the milkweed plant. He is careful so the caterpillars do not fall on the ground. I put the milkweed and caterpillars into my bag.

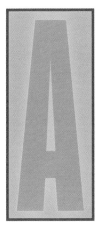 t home we put the milkweed and the caterpillars in a big jar on the mantel. "All we have to do is give them plenty of fresh milkweed," says Papa, "and wait. Pretty soon you will see a miracle."

**E**very day I look at the caterpillars. They are always eating. I jump up and down. "When will it happen, Papa? Will the miracle happen today?"

"Be patient," says Papa. "Sometimes miracles take time."

One day I see a strange thing in the caterpillar jar. One caterpillar is missing. And there is a bright green sack hanging from a milkweed stem. A green sack with beautiful gold spots.

Papa cuts off the section of stem where the green sack is. He is careful not to touch the sack. "This is a chrysalis," he tells me as he tapes the piece of stem to the top of the doorway. "The caterpillar is inside it. It is part of the miracle."

very day I look at the chrysalis. But it just hangs there. I wonder if the caterpillar can see out. I wonder if he can see me down here looking up.

his morning the beautiful green-and-gold chrysalis is dark. It isn't very pretty anymore at all. "What's wrong?" I shout to Papa.

Papa comes to look at the chrysalis. He smiles. "You will see the rest of the miracle very soon," he says.

he chrysalis is opening. Something is coming out! It has long, long, thin black legs and crumpled-up wings. It is a butterfly! A butterfly is being born!

**P**apa gently touches the butterfly's foot. The butterfly moves onto Papa's finger. It hangs there upside down. "Let's go outside," Papa says.

The butterfly's wings wave slowly back and forth in the sunshine. They are getting bigger and smoother. They are not all crumpled up anymore. Suddenly I laugh. "Look, Papa! The butterfly is sticking out its tongue!"

apa and I sit on the warm grass. The butterfly is crawling on my finger. Its tiny feet tickle my skin. Papa says it will soon be ready to fly away.

"You have seen a miracle of change," says Papa. "God took that little black-and-yellow caterpillar and changed it into a beautiful butterfly. It's a lot like what He is doing inside of you. He is making you beautiful on the inside."

"You mean I have beautiful bones?" I ask Papa.

"Of course, you have beautiful bones!" Papa's eyes laugh at me. "But I'm talking about your heart. The real you inside you. The Bible tells us that when we ask Him, God changes our stubborn, sinful hearts into loving, obedient hearts. He puts His Spirit inside us. He makes us beautiful in the inside."

uddenly, my butterfly spreads its wings and flies away. We watch it flutter across the yard and land in the lilac tree.

hank You, God, for changing my heart and making me more like You.

Don't stop, God. Don't stop making miracles inside me.

Parent's Guide

Share God's Transforming Power With Your Child

❖ You and your child can do what David and his papa did—watch caterpillars turn into butterflies. There are books to help you know how to do this.

❖ Talk with your child about how he is changing. Keep a record of his growth on a growth chart. Make a tradition out of measuring him regularly.

❖ Go through the family picture album with your child. Tell her what she was like at the ages she was in each picture. Remark how she has changed not only in size, but in behavior. Say things like,"You used to bite people when you were two. I had to teach you that biting hurts other people, and now you don't do it anymore." Don't put her down for how she used to be, but do remark on her progress.

❖ Children are very conscious of outside differences in people (and will often point them out in such a way as to embarrass their parents). Tell your child that for Jesus, what is on the inside is much more important than what is on the outside. That's why Jesus is helping us grow beautiful on the inside.

❖ Cut out some bone-shaped pieces of paper and use them to record beautiful actions done in your family. Put the bones where everyone can see them—perhaps on the refrigerator. Ask every day if there is another bone that can be put up. Comment frequently on how Jesus is helping you become beautiful inside. In family prayer, ask for Jesus' power to keep changing you. Thank Him for the changes you've been able to record.

❖ The steps in accepting Jesus as our personal Saviour—sometimes called being converted—are described more fully in the parent's guide in the back of *Rescued From the River!*, book two in this series.

❖ The miracle of becoming beautiful on the inside—another facet of conversion—happens over the course of a lifetime. But all the while God is helping us change, He also sees us as perfect because our sinfulness is covered by His Son's life. By accepting our children with love and patience and seeing them as beautiful, we convey to them the love and acceptance of God. The knowledge of His acceptance is one of the most important gifts we can give our children.

Linda Porter Carlyle and Aileen Andres Sox

Books by Linda Porter Carlyle

I Can Choose
A Child's Steps to Jesus

God and Joseph and Me	*Cookies in the Mailbox*
Rescued From the River!	*Beautiful Bones and Butterflies*
Grandma Stepped on Fred!	*No Olives Tonight!*
Max Moves In	*Happy Birthday Tomorrow to Me!*